A DISNEY Adventures BOOK

DINO files
UNEARTHED

BY ANDREW RAGAN

DISNEY PRESS
New York

May '98

To Alvin, Vivian, Zachary &
Jeremiah,

I know you're all a bit old
for this, but maybe you'll
have some little dino-phobe
visitors sometime. Hope to
see you this summer. Andy

PHOTO CREDITS
Illustrations by Bob McMacken
Front cover photographs: courtesy of Bob London (top) and Archive Photos (bottom). Back
cover photographs: courtesy of Archive Photos (top and bottom) and the Museum of the
Rockies (bottom right).

Interior: p. iii (bottom): courtesy of Sygma; p. 67: courtesy of Archive Photos; pp. 57, 59, 60,
63, 65: courtesy of Matrix; pp. iii (middle), 52: courtesy of the Royal Tyrrell Museum
Library; pp. 43, 45, 46: courtesy of PhotoDisk; pp. iii (top), 1, 61: courtesy of the Museum of
the Rockies.

Printed in the United States of America.

First Edition
1 3 5 7 9 10 8 6 4 2

The text for this book is set in 14-point Mrs. Eaves.

ISBN: 0-7868-4207-5 (paperback)

Library of Congress Catalog Card Number: 97-80158

For more Disney Press fun, visit www.DisneyBooks.com

CONTENTS

WELCOME TO THE DINO FILES!

Every six or seven weeks, some fossil hunter somewhere digs up the bones of a brand-new dinosaur. Often it's not even someone on the lookout for old bones, but a hiker, camper, or a

kid like you, just doing your own thing.

But dinosaur news is always *big* news—as if you didn't already know that. There just aren't a whole lot of things as huge, as wild, as weird, and as scary as these beasts who ruled the Earth—devouring plants and each other—for 150 million years.

In this book, we've gathered the coolest information out there about dinosaurs. Who knows when you might need it? On a dig with your best buds. When you bump into a famous dino-hunter at the video store. Or to prep for an expedition to your favorite museum. You just never know. . . .

Chapter 1

WHEN DINOS RULED

Dinosaurs came along way before we humans ever showed up on Earth. And they were around *a lot* longer, too. Our measly 500,000 years of hanging out are a blink in time compared to 150 million years of stomping around.

Not that all dinosaurs partied on Earth at the same time. Different dinos lived during three main eras:

The Triassic Period
250 to 208 million years ago

Reptiles had been skulking around already for 100 million years, and amphibians and fish a lot longer than that. About 228 million years ago, the first dinos hit the scene. Back then, all the Earth's land was smooshed together into one super-continent called *Pangaea* (pan-JEE-uh). (That's why bones of the same dinos are sometimes found on different continents today.)

The first dinos weren't as huge and fearsome as later ones, but they weren't pushovers, either. The dog-sized meat eater *Eoraptor* ("dawn stealer"), the oldest dino found so far, was one. *Plateosaurus* ("flat lizard"), fore-runner of giants like *Brachiosaurus*, starred in the Trias-sic. And so did vicious *Coelophysis*.

The earliest relatives of mammals were shrewlike little guys that showed up in the Triassic age, as well.

The Jurassic Period
208 to 146 million years ago

You know it from the movies. The experts know it as the time the super-continent began cracking up, and dinosaurs became humongous, wild, and crazy.

Jurassic forests sprouted super-tall trees such as the redwoods. In order to munch their needles, some

The experts know it as the time the super-continent began cracking up, and dinosaurs became humongous, wild, and crazy.

dinos grew to match the height of the trees. You may have heard of them: *Apatosaurus, Brachiosaurus,* and *Seismosaurus.*

Certain dinos were also trying out newfangled wings, clearing the air for modern birds. Then there were the sometimes-flapping hang gliders of Jurassic days—the winged pterosaurs. They weren't dinos at all, though they did have the same ancestors and hung out in the same era. We can't forget *Stegosaurus,* with its weird plates. And we had better mention *Allosaurus,* the flesh eater who paved the way for monsters such as *T. rex.*

The Cretaceous Period
146 to 65 million years ago

The heyday of dinos. The continents were splitting further, and more kinds of dinosaurs than ever before roamed the Earth. Some were downright bizarre, like

Triceratops, Euoplocephalus, Parasaurolophus, and *Pachycephalosaurus.*

This was also the time of the most ferocious dinos ever: *Velociraptor, Baryonyx,* and big, bad *Tyrannosaurus rex.* In fact, new discoveries are proving that these monsters weren't the only extreme bone-crunchers of the age.

The end of the Cretaceous was also the end of the line for almost all the dinosaurs. But some scientists are certain that dinos lived on—in the form of birds!

Chapter 2

MEET THE MONSTERS

In case you don't already know it, "dinosaur" is another way of saying "terrible lizard." After their bones started popping up all over Europe, that's what British scientist Sir Richard Owen first named the big critters in 1841.

Turns out that dinosaurs aren't really lizards. But some of them *are* terrible. *T. rex* comes to mind. And the vicious raptors. But are you up on the *latest* dino scoop? Or the weirdest? If not, read on. . . .

"DECEPTIVE LIZARD"

Officially known as: *Apatosaurus* (a-PAT-o-SORE-us)

A.k.a.: "Pat," "Whip-it," "*Brontosaurus*"

Card-carrying member of: The Sauropod clan

Days of Thunder: Late Jurassic, 150–140 million years ago

Attitude: Easygoing, but a little confused

If it could talk: "Finally, I have my head on straight."

Athletic profile:

Weight: 35 tons

Length: 90 feet (27 m)—half of that was its tail

Speed: 4 mph (6.4 kph) on four legs

Best move: the Whip, Claw, and Stomp

Where Do They Get Those Names?

Ever wonder why so many dinosaur names twist your tongue into 50 million knots? It's because paleontologists (pay-lee-on-TOL-ah-jists) often borrow words or word parts from the ancient Latin and Greek languages to name dinos. Actually, scientists the world over have used these languages to name all sorts of plants and animals. This way, a plant or animal—or dinosaur—ends up with the same scientific name everywhere, so there's no confusion.

Scientific names sometimes work like secret codes. Scientists try to tell something about the species through the names they choose. Take *Maiasaura*, for example. *Maia* means "good mother," and *saura* means "lizard." That tells you a lot about what kind of dinosaur *Maiasaura* was. (Find out more about *Maiasaura* on p. 34.)

There are no real rules, however, about naming new dinos. Dino-hunter Dr. Bob Bakker, for example, named one of his newest discoveries *Drinker* after *his* favorite old-time dino-hunting hero, Edward Drinker Cope. (See pages 58 and 66.)

Recommended sport: basketball (under the boards)

Brains: Tiny as a kitten's

Chow time: Pat stretched its super-long neck to nibble leaves and needles off the highest trees. Its teeth were peg-shaped and worked like a rake.

Lethal weapons: Pat could crush you with its tree-

The Tail's the Tale

The *Apatosaurus* in New York's American Museum of Natural History got more than a headgear makeover in 1991. New vertebrae lengthened its neck to 20 feet (6 m). And, with a bunch of new bones added on, its tail grew to 44 feet (13 m). (Total tally of tail bones: 82. Humans have 206 bones altogether.) The tail-without-an-end, carried off the ground, helped Pat balance its long neck.

trunk limbs and great weight. Or slash you with the single huge claw on each of its front feet (mostly used for digging up grub). Or swipe you with its 44-foot (13 m) long tail—half the length of a basketball court. (But that's only if you got Pat *real* mad—it was normally happy-go-lucky.)

Digs: Western United States

Claim to fame: The big name-and-noggin mix-up. Turns out two look-alike skeletons of gigantic plant eaters were dug up out West in the late 1870s and given different names: *Apatosaurus* and *Brontosaurus*. But they were really the same model. By the time experts figured this out, *Brontosaurus* was the fave name tag. Now museums are switching back to "Pat," since the A-name was officially used first. (No wonder the name means "deceptive lizard.")

And if you think *that's* confusing . . . Pat's original

skeletons seemed at first to have no skulls. Rather, the skulls dug up nearby seemed way too small for Pat's big bod. So a famous old-time dino expert stuck the larger skull of *Camarasaurus*, another big plant muncher, onto Pat's neck. Most museums copied him, and Pat sported Cammy's head for nearly a century.

Finally, dino sleuth Jack McIntosh dug up some old files and older bones from different museums to come up with Pat's proper pate. And now, in museums everywhere, Pat is having both its head—and its name—put on straight.

Compare!

To give you an idea of just how big (or small) dinosaurs were, check out the stats of these still-living critters:

• The African elephant is the largest land animal. It averages 10 1/2 feet tall (3 m) and 5 1/2 tons.

• The biggest mammal alive today, the blue whale, can stretch 110 feet (33 m) and can weigh 130 tons.

• The giraffe is the tallest mammal alive. A Masai giraffe can reach heights of 17 feet (5 m).

"ANCIENT WING"

Officially known as: *Archaeopteryx* (ark-ee-OP-ter-ix)

A.k.a.: "Arkie," "Wings," "Flygirl"

Card-carrying member of: The Theropod clan

Days on the wing: Early Cretaceous, 150 million years ago

Attitude: A little flighty

If it could talk: "Let's wing it."

Athletic profile:

Weight: 1–2 pounds (.4–.9 kg)

The claws on its wings and feet could inflict serious damage, and you wouldn't want it to mistake your fingers for a worm.

Length: 1 foot (.3 m)

Special f/x: Feathery wings tipped with triple claws, not to mention its clawed toes. Some experts figure this dino bird clawed its way up trees and then set sail from branches. Its wing muscles weren't heavy-duty, so it may have glided mostly, with a flap here and there.

Best move: the Swoop

Recommended sport: hang gliding

Sensory check: Great bird's-eye views

Brains: A real birdbrain. (In dino terms, that means BIG. Arkie was a quick-witted critter.)

Chow time: Arkie probably used its air time to snag flying insects, which may be why this crow-sized character sprouted feathers and wings in the first place. Unlike today's feathered friends, Arkie brandished a mouthful of tiny, sharp teeth that could have been for mincing bugs or fish—nobody's quite sure.

Lethal weapon: The claws on its wings and feet could inflict serious damage, and you wouldn't want it to mistake your fingers for a worm. But the real danger: bird droppings.

Digs: Southern Germany

Claim to fame: It's a bird! It's a dinosaur! No, it's *Archaeopteryx*! Arkie is one of the rarest, most complete, and most priceless fossils in the world. It's also one of the most important, since very few fossils show off feathers. In fact, Arkie has so many features of both birds and dinosaurs that some scientists aren't sure exactly *what* it is. Like a dino, it has teeth and a long,

Birds of a Feather?

Don't look now, but a dinosaur may be building a nest in your backyard. Okay, okay, so it's not *T. rex*. But more and more dino experts are convinced that sparrows, robins, and other birds are the great-great-great-great-grandchildren of dinosaurs. They say that small meat-munching dinos—such as *Coelophysis* (p. 23)—bear an uncanny resemblance to today's winged wonders. Their bones are hollow. They stand upright on two back feet. And those feet have three claws.

What does all this mean? For one thing, scientists can learn a lot about dino behavior just by watching their bird feeders. We mammals are way outnumbered by a bunch of winged "dinosaurs"! There are about 4,000 types of mammals—and 9,000 kinds of birds!

bony tail. But like a bird, it has wings, feathers, perching feet, and birdlike eyes and brains. (It even has a wishbone!) Some scientists think of Arkie as a dinosaur in the process of evolving into a bird—and one piece of proof that all birds today are the super-great-grandchildren of dinosaurs.

"HEAVY CLAW"

Officially known as: Baryonyx (BA-ree-ON-ix)
A.k.a.: "Claws," "Fishbreath," "Grizzly Bary"

Card-carrying member of: The Theropod Clan
Gone fishing: Early Cretaceous, 125 million years ago
Attitude: Laid-back—until it comes to fishing. Then it's ruthless.
If it could talk: "What's biting?"
Athletic profile:

Weight: 2 tons
Height: 13 1/2 feet (4 m)
Length: 33 feet (9.9 m)
Speed: quick, in short sprints
Best move: the Hook

A Rocky Stomach

Turns out that *Seismosaurus*—and a lot of other large plant-munching dinos—couldn't digest its veggies (not without a little help, anyway). Dino experts dug up 240 walnut-sized stones (called *gastroliths*) near Seismo's big belly. Seismo's tiny teeth were great for plucking leaves off tall trees, but not much good for chewing them up. The rocks helped grind the greens inside Seismo's tummy.

Recommended sport: professional angling

Sensory check: Sharp enough eyes to spy fish in the water. Long, crocodilelike snout suggests a decent sniffer.

Lethal weapons: 12-inch-long killer claws, one on each hand. Fossilized fish scales were found in its stomach, so experts figure Claws used its frightening fingers to snag fish in the water, much like grizzly bears do today.

Chow time: Each side of Claws's lower jaw had 32 saw-edged teeth (twice as many as most other meat eaters). The top jaw held a few, as well. All those choppers put the clamp on what-

Claws may also have nosed deep into decaying carcasses for extra treats.

ever Claws hooked for dinner. Claws may also have nosed deep into decaying carcasses for extra treats. (Its long snout and high-up nostrils would've let it breathe easily, despite the stink.) Parts of an *Iguanodon* were also found in its belly.

Digs: Britain. Similar jaws and claws found in western Africa.

Claim to fame: The experts don't usually expect to find much more than busted-up dino pieces in picked-over Britain. But plumber and amateur fossil hunter William J. Walker surprised them all in 1983. That's when he visited a clay quarry outside of London and dug up Fishbreath's monster claw. This lucky strike led to the almost complete skeleton of *Baryonyx*, the fishing dino meat eater that no one had ever heard of before. In fact, the second part of *Baryonyx's* official name is *walkeri*, after Mr. Walker.

"ARM LIZARD"

Officially known as: *Brachiosaurus* (BRACK-ee-oh-SORE-us)

A.k.a.: "Bracky," "Stretch"

Card-carrying member of: The Sauropod clan

Weighty days: Late Jurassic/early Cretaceous, 150– 130 million years ago

Attitude: Gentle giant with a humongous heart. (Really, its ticker had to be enormous to supply blood to that bulky body.)

If it could talk: "Pain in the neck? I'll tell you about a pain in the neck."

Athletic profile:
Weight: 80 tons, maybe more
Height: 54 feet (16 m)

Length: 82.5 feet
(25 m)
Speed: 2—4 mph
(3.2—6.4 kph) on four legs
Best move: the Dunk-and-Squash
Recommended sport: Sumo-basketball

Would you attack a monster as massive as 14 large elephants?

Brains: Walnut-sized noodle in an 80-ton body. Doesn't take a genius to figure *that* I.Q.

Chow time: Bracky's stretch-neck let it nibble leaves off trees as tall as four-story buildings, where few other dinos could butt in. (That's at least twice as high as a giraffe's reach.) Good thing, too—it had to munch veggies *all day long* to fuel that humongous bod. Its tiny, chisel-shaped teeth were great leaf pluckers, but not much good for chewing.

Lethal weapon: Its SIZE. Would you attack a monster as massive as 14 large elephants?

Digs: Western United States, Africa, and Portugal

Claim to fame: For a while there, Bracky starred as the world's most humongous dinosaur—not to mention land animal—ever. It's lost the BIGGEST title (see "Make Room at the Top . . . ," p. 21.), but it's still the Mount Everest of all complete dinos on view in muse-

Make Room at the Top . . . Lots of Room

Dino-size-wise, no critter could touch Bracky for nearly eight decades. Then, in 1979, a Utah fossil digger called "Dinosaur Jim Jenson" came up with the 9-foot-long (2.7 m) shoulder blade of *Ultrasaurus* ("Beyond Lizard"), the biggest single dino bone ever found.

Bracky's heavyweight title was in trouble.

Based on guesses from just a few of its bones, "Ultra" may have stretched 100 feet (30 m) from neck to tail—as long as three schoolbuses. A ride on top of its head—50 feet (15 m) up—would let you peek into windows of six-story-high buildings. And a giraffe could stroll between Ultra's legs—without ducking.

If all that wasn't enough, the experts figure Ultra weighed in at 130 tons—the weight of more than twenty elephants! No wonder some paleontologists rank *Ultrasaurous* as the largest land animal ever.

Then again, some don't. Also in '79, hikers in New Mexico stumbled upon the bones of *Seismosaurus*. The "earthshaking lizard" measures more than 150 feet (45 m) from snout to tail. At half the length of a football field, that makes "Seismo" the longest dinosaur to date.

The final stats for Ultra and Seismo aren't all in yet. But both are great candidates for the title of Most Humongous. Then again, maybe in the meantime you'll stumble upon even bigger bones.

ums. A 74-foot (22 m) *Brachiosaurus*, the whoppingest dino ever pieced together, kisses the ceiling at the Natural History Museum of Humboldt University in Berlin, Germany. (You can also see one close to that size at Chicago's Field Museum.)

"HOLLOW BONE"

Officially known as: *Coelophysis* (see-LOW-fye-siss)

A.k.a.: "C-low," "Cannibal," *"Rioarribasaurus"* (its newest scientific name)

Card-carry-ing member of: The Theropod clan

Gourmet days: Late Triassic, 200 million years ago

Attitude: Feisty, with a sharp bite

If it could talk: "Honey, I ate the kids."

Athletic profile:

Weight: 70 pounds

Length: 6–8 feet (1.8– 2.4 m)

Speed: lightning quick on two back legs

Special f/x: this sleek, nimble-footed dino ran like a bird on three of its four toes and used its long, slender tail to keep its balance.

Its nastiest trick was the pack attack, when it ganged up on bigger dinos.

Best move: the Quick Bite

Recommended sport: Ultimate Frisbee

Sensory check: Super vision for eyeing up dinner

Brains: Pretty bright, for one of the oldest dinos ever found

Chow time: Chased down lizards and smaller critters, then snagged them with its triple-clawed hands. Its 80 saw-edged teeth did the carving. (See "Claim to fame" for more on its diet.)

Lethal weapons: Its teeth and claws were deadly enough, but C-low's nastiest trick was the pack attack, when it ganged up on bigger dinos. At one spectacular dig called Ghost Ranch in New Mexico, more than 1,000 *Coelophysis* skeletons have been found. Multiply *that* by 80 teeth per mouth, and you get the gruesome picture.

Digs: Southwestern United States

Claim to fame: When *Coelophysis* ran out of lizards for lunch, it snapped up the next closest thing: its own babies! Dino experts guess this because tiny C-low skeletons have been found at Ghost Ranch near what would have been the stomachs of several *Coelophysis* adults.

"TRUE-PLATED HEAD"

Officially known as: *Euoplocephalus* (you-oh-plo-SEF-alus)

A.k.a.: "The Club," "Tank," "Bam-Bam"

Card-carrying member of: The Ankylosaur clan

Clubbing days: Late Cretaceous era, 70–65 million years ago

Attitude: A little shy under all its armor. But a bruiser if you get pushy.

If it could talk: "Heads you lose; tails I win."

Athletic profile:

Weight: 2–3 tons

Height: 5 feet (1.5 m) at the hips (but no pushover)

Wasn't much you could do to hurt the Club—unless you could flip 'em over: its belly was its soft spot.

Length: 15–20 feet (4.5–6 m)

Speed: S-L-O-W, maybe 3 mph (4.8 kph) on four feet

Best move: the Club-Swing.

Recommended sport: baseball (as designated hitter)

Sensory check: Excellent sniffer

Brains: Tiny and S-L-O-W

Chow time: Used rounded snout and wide beak for plucking soft, ground-level green things, though stubby cheek choppers weren't the best for chewing. May have had a hi-tech tummy beneath its armor to help break down leathery leaves.

Lethal weapons: Three-foot-wide (.9 m) monster club at the end of its tail that looked like huge boulders lashed together. One home-run swing with this sledge-hammer could crush the kneecaps of even mighty *T. rex*. You wouldn't want to land on the Club's back, either: it bristled with sharp spikes.

Weakness: Wasn't much you could do to hurt the Club—unless you could flip 'em over: its belly was its soft spot. Like a turtle on its back, the Club had trouble flipping itself back over.

Digs: Western Canada

Claim to fame: *Euoplocephalus* was a living suit of armor—the medieval knight of the dino world. Hunks of bone and tough sheaths of horn covered almost every part of it. Its skull, a rock-hard helmet, even had built-in eyelid coverings. With all that weight, the Club was surprisingly nimble. Thanks to a lack of tail track fossils, experts figure that it carried its heavy club in the air and swung it using flexible, super-powerful butt muscles.

"THICK-HEADED LIZARD"

Officially known as: *Pachycephalosaurus* (PAK-ee-SEF-ah-low-SORE-us)

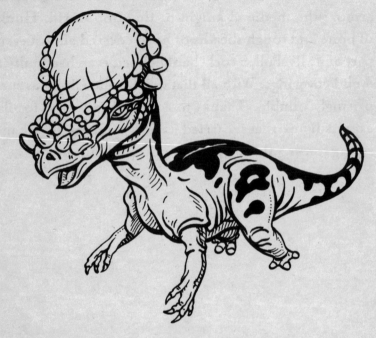

A.k.a.: "Butthead," "Crash," "Bone-dome"

Card-carrying member of: The Ornithopod clan

Head-banging days: Late Cretaceous era, 70–65 million years ago

Attitude: Pleasant enough, but could be thick-headed about some things

If it could talk: "Heads I win; tails you lose."

Athletic profile:

Weight: 15 tons

Height: 7 feet (2 m) on two legs

Length: 15 feet (4.5 m)

Best move: the Head Butt

Recommended sport: football (offensive tackle)

Sensory check: Good eyes, good nose

Brains: No bigger than a chicken egg—but lots of protection

Chow time: Dug up roots and bugs with its short forelimbs; munched them with tiny, sharp teeth.

Lethal weapon: A bony, 12-inch-thick skull—the heaviest-duty headgear of any dino. Also sported a crown of knobs and bumps around its dome, and a few on its snout for good measure. A head butt with this

Crash-Test Dummies

Pachycephalosaurus was one dino whose head did not crack under pressure—even if it came from butting it with another foot-thick (.3 m) Bone-dome. But how did the rest of its body handle the shock? The experts figure Bone-dome had super-strong neck muscles. It also might have had a special neck joint that crumpled up—for a moment—before straightening out again, as good as new.

noggin would feel like being bounced off a ton of bricks.

Digs: Western North America

Claim to fame: "Butthead" was the battering ram of dino days. It likely used its thick skull against other bone domes to settle who was boss of the herd—and who got to mate.

"BESIDE RIDGE LIZARD"

Officially known as: *Parasaurolophus* (PARA-sore-oh-LOFF-us). You'd think a dino with a head like this would have its own cool name to go along with it. But *Parasaurolophus* got its scientific tag because it looks a bit like its dino cousin, *Saurolophus*, or "Ridge Lizard."

A.k.a.: "Honker," "Bugle-brain"

Card-carrying member of: The Ornithopod clan

Jazz-playing era: Late Cretaceous, 80–65 million years ago

Attitude: Proud—definitely liked to toot its own horn

If it could talk: "Honk if you love me."

Athletic profile:

Weight: 3–4 tons

Height: 16 feet (4.8 m) on two legs

Length: 30 feet (9 m)

Speed: fast, on two feet

Special f/x (besides its head horn): Its big tail was flat-sided, like a fish's, and its hands were paddle-shaped.

Best move: the Bellow

Recommended activity: marching band

A Great Impression

It's hard enough finding dino bones. Imagine coming across a fossil showing what dino skin looked like! That's what happened to old-time dino hunter Charles H. Sternberg in the early 1900s. He was looking for dino bones in Kansas when he found the mummy of *Edmontosaurus*, a hadrosaur. It had likely been caught in a sandstorm. The sand preserved a perfect impression of the dinosaur's skin, which looks like the bumpy surface of a basketball!

Members of the Band

Honker wasn't the only member of its extended family, called the hadrosaurs (or "duckbills"), who could carry a tune. Each of its musical cousins had a unique "instrument" perched on its head. *Tsintosaurus*, from Asia, wore a unicornlike headpiece that may have supported an inflatable nose balloon to help it croon. *Corythosaurus* sported headware shaped like a handheld fan. Forty-nine-foot-long (14.7 m) *Labeosaurus*, with its spike-and-blade helmet, was the duckbill with the weirdest crest. And *Saurolophus*'s single head-spike may also have been connected to a blow-up skin flap on its schnoz. The largest hadrosaur, *Shantungosaurus*, must have been the band's road manager: it had no crest at all. Another crestless duckbill, *Anatosaurus*, had the most back teeth of any duckbill—more than 1,400 of 'em.

Sensory check: Slick eardrums (built into the sides of its head) were excellent for tuning in the songs of other bugle-brains. Keen eyesight and sniffing power, too.

Brains: Fairly smart for a dino, with an especially good head for music. Hard to beat at "Name that tune."

Chow time: Its toothless, ducky beak tore off tough veggies such as leaves, pine needles, and twigs. Then its powerful jaws, packed with *hundreds* of diamond-shaped teeth, ground the greens to a pulp.

Lethal weapon: Okay, so maybe it wasn't lethal—but

the blast from Honker's head horn would probably scare the heck out of you. If nothing else, it warned other honkers of danger. (See "Claim to fame" below.)

Digs: Western North America

Claim to fame: Honker had a bony crest curving back from its skull as long as a full-grown person. For a while, dino experts thought hollow tubes inside the crest let Honker and similar dinos breathe underwater, the way a snorkel works. But now most think the tubes operated more like a trombone. They allowed Honker to belch loud and low to mate, send out warning signals, and gossip with its pals. Paleontologist David Weishampel of Johns Hopkins University even built a plastic model of Honker's horn to imitate the dino's sounds. What's

A Good Mama?

Maiasaura means "Good Mother Lizard." And no wonder. A huge nesting site of this large duckbill has been uncovered in Montana by dino diggers. Fossils of big *Maiasaura* lie right next to 6-foot-wide (1.8 m) nests full of *Maiasaura* eggs, hatchlings, and even some kids. This proved for the first time that some dinos cared for their eggs and loved their young 'uns enough to stay close to their nests. The adults must have liked each other, too. One Montana dig is the graveyard of at least 10,000 *Maiasaura*. (For more on *Maiasaura*, see p. 9.)

more, Honker's crest is going hi-tech. Scientists in Albuquerque, New Mexico, are running the dino's skull through electronic imaging machines to map out its airways. With that info, computers will try for an even closer rendition of Honker's greatest hits.

They allowed Honker to belch loud and low to mate, send out warning signals, and gossip with its pals.

"ROOFED REPTILE"

Officially known as: *Stegosaurus* (steg-oh-SORE-us)
A.k.a.: "Plates," "Steggie," "Mohawk"

Card-carrying member of: The Stegosaur clan
Dishing days: Late Jurassic, 150—140 million years ago
Attitude: Grumpy—but won't bother you if you don't bother it

If it could talk: "Duh."

Athletic profile:

Weight: 2 tons

Height: 11 1/2 feet (3.5 m) to its highest plate

Length: 20–25 feet (6–7.5 m)

Best move: the Spike-Whip

Recommended sport: tennis (try to get a ball past *those* rackets!)

Brains: Tiny, narrow skull held a noodle no bigger than a golf ball. But who's calling Steggie stupid? This dino was a huge success on Earth for *10 million years*!

Chow time: Its narrow, toothless beak snipped low-growing ferns and other veggies. Tiny munchers in back chewed 'em up. Might have swallowed rocks to help mulch the veggies even more inside its belly.

Lethal weapon: Two wicked pairs of sharp, 4-foot-

Just Don't Put Them in the Dishwasher

Stegosaurus's plates weren't attached to its skeleton—they just grew right out of its skin. And besides keeping Steggie cool—or warm—they may have served other purposes. Some scientists think the plates were covered with horn, a fingernail-like material, as were its tail spikes, for more protection against meat eaters. Others say they glowed in Technicolor to show off age or to impress a date.

long (1.2 m) spikes planted on the end of a power-packed tail. One flick of its tail could tear open the tummy of even the meanest meat chomper sniffing too close.

Digs: Western North America

Claim to fame: After Steggie was first dug up, scientists put her back together with the plates lying flat on her back, like roof shingles. (Now you know why she's called the "roofed reptile.") Later, the experts stood the plates up. They guessed that the large discs helped heat and cool off the big dino. Some think blood vessels and skin covered the plates. When the plates caught some rays, Steggie warmed up all over. When they caught a breeze, she cooled right down. And no wonder: the largest plates measured 3 feet (.9 m) across. Scientists still aren't sure *how* the plates were lined up: staggered, in pairs, or overlapping. But the newest evidence points to a single row straight down the spine.

"THREE-HORNED FACE"

Officially known as: *Triceratops* (try-SERRA-tops)
A.k.a.: "Spikes," "Cement Truck," "Rhino-dino"

Card-carrying member of: The Ceratopsian clan
Roaming days: Late Cretaceous era, 70–65 million years ago
Attitude: On the prickly side
If it could talk: "You scratch my back, I'll scratch yours."

Big-Head

. . . And the winner for the largest frill—and the largest skull—of any land animal ever is . . . *Torosaurus*! From the point of its beak to the edge of its frilly-frill-frill, Toro's noggin measured 8 1/2 feet (2.5 m)! That's longer than the tallest pro basketball player is tall.

Athletic profile:

Weight: 4.5–6 tons

Height: 10 feet (3 m) at the hips

Length: 30 feet (9 m)

Speed: 10–15 mph (16–24 kph)

Best move: the Charge

Recommended sports: football (nose tackle)

Sensory check: Its eyeballs alone were the size of baseballs—but no surprise: its head could weigh 2,000 pounds!

Brains: A bit of a numbskull

Chow time: Had no front teeth—just a parrotlike beak for snipping tough palm leaves and other stringy plants. In back, a jaw full of choppers like grass shears finished off the job.

Lethal weapons: Its looks—if looks could kill. This beast sported more than 3-foot-long (.9 m) bayonets for eyebrows, a horned nose, and a gigantic armored frill, or neck shield. These four-footed brutes likely hung out in herds, like buffalo. When a hungry meat chomper came sniffing around, Spikes and his pals may have formed a circle with their heads—and

Its eyeballs alone were the size of baseballs.

horns—facing outward. The kids would hide inside the circle. (Cool fort.)

Digs: Western United States and Canada; earlier versions found in eastern Asia

Claim to fame: Largest, heftiest, and most commonly found of the horned dinos. Even though another horn-head had a longer frill, *Triceratops*'s 6-foot (1.8 m) neck shield was, unlike most others, solid as a rock. Its 3-foot (.9 m) eyebrow horns were also the longest spikes to adorn any frill. Old "three-horned-head" was one of the last dinos to bite the dust when all of the others went belly-up.

"WOUNDING TOOTH"

Officially known as: *Troodon* (TROH-ah-don)
A.k.a.: "Cretaceous Coyote," "Einstein," *"Stenony-*

chosaurus" (its old scientific name)
   Card-carrying member of: The Theropod clan
   Days of deep thoughts: Late Cretaceous era, 70–65
million years ago
   Attitude: Wise-guy
   If it could talk: "Checkmate."
   Athletic profile:
Weight: 60 pounds (25 kg)

Length: 6 feet (1.8 m), nose-to-tail

Speed: fast and nimble, 25–30 mph (40–48 kph) on two feet

Special f/x: tail kept it balanced on the run and helped it turn on a dime.

Best move: Grab-and-Run

Recommended sport: flag football (quarterback or wide receiver)

Sensory check: Huge eyes for its size, aimed straight ahead—excellent for seeing at night and judging what was close or far.

Chow time: Three long, sharp-clawed fingers on each hand could snatch small mammals or reptiles and hold them, like few other dinos. (The fingers were opposable, like human thumbs.) Its tiny triangular teeth were smaller than human molars—but saw-edged, for slicing into flesh. Loved to eat out at night.

> If its smarts and speed and fingers didn't get you, its large, sicklelike toe-claws would.

Brains: For the size of its skull, this creature had the biggest brain in dino-land. A head-of-the-class act.

Lethal weapons: If its smarts and speed and fingers didn't get you, its large, sicklelike toe claws would. They stuck out on the second toe of each foot. Not only that: these meat eaters may have traveled in *packs*.

Digs: Western United States, Canada, Mongolia, and China

Claim to fame: Besides its brains, Einstein is known for the air pockets in its bones. That made it super-light and birdlike. In fact, birds are the only creatures alive today with similar airy skeletons.

Dino-person?

Quick: What stands upright on two feet, has big eyes and grasping fingers, and is reasonably intelligent? Humans, you say? That's one answer. Another is *Troodon.* This idea got Dale Russell, fossil curator at the Canadian Museum of Nature in Ottawa, wondering. If dinosaurs hadn't died out millions of years ago, could a "smart" one such as *Troodon* have evolved into an intelligent, humanlike creature? With so many humanoid traits already in place, Russell figures Einstein might well have been on its way. He and his staff even built a model of what a dino-person might have looked like. (Think of an overgrown "ET.") Its name: "Dinosauroid."

"KING OF THE TYRANT LIZARDS"

Officially known as: *Tyrannosaurus rex* (tie-RAN-oh-SORE-us REX)

A.k.a.: "T. rex," "The King," "Boss"

Card-carrying member of: The Theropod clan

Days of rage: Late Cretaceous era, 70–65 million years ago

Attitude: Really, really nasty—and that's on a good day

If it could talk: Wouldn't have to.

Athletic profile:

Weight: 6 tons

Height: 18 feet (5.4 m)

Length: 40 feet (12 m)

Speed: up to 40 mph (64 kph) on two feet

Best move: the Chomp

Recommended sport: Extreme Fighting (no rules)

Sensory check: Beady little eyes (for such a big guy), but sharp as an eagle's. Could sniff out a meal a mile away. Plus hi-fi hearing.

Brains: Small noodle for a noggin up to 5 feet (1.5 m) long, but no dummy

Chow time: Ate *any* animal, dead or alive. Favorite feast: two-footed veggie eaters. Needed to eat its own weight in meat every week.

Lethal weapons: Sixty curved, jagged-edged, 7-inch fangs in a 3-foot-wide (.9 m) power jaw. Excellent for slicing and dicing flesh, or for crunching through ribs, shoulder blades, and skulls. Its jaw was twice as powerful as most other predators'. Massive hind legs, feet way

Don't Stand Up So Straight!

T. rex and other big meat eaters have been getting a major tail-lift in museums around the globe. Turns out they didn't stomp around dragging their tails as most experts thought. (How do they know? No tail tracks!) More likely they bent forward, stalking low to the ground like chickens. They'd balance themselves with their uplifted tails.

bigger than Shaquille O'Neal's, and huge, hawklike toe claws.

Digs: Western United States and Canada; possibly Mongolia, in Asia

Claim to fame: Biggest, baddest monster ever with a taste for raw flesh and bones in North America—or maybe the world. Could swallow a whole horse—not to mention a person—in one bite.

"SPEEDY THIEF"

Officially known as: *Velociraptor* (VEL-oh-si-RAP-tor)
A.k.a.: "Vicious Velly," "Hollywood," "Hawk-claw"

Card-carrying member of: The Theropod clan

Fast times: Late Cretaceous, 85–80 million years ago

Attitude: Always looking for the limelight. Known to stab other dinos in the back—or the front. Definitely not nice.

If it could speak: "Talk to my agent."

Athletic profile:

Size: 6 feet (1.8 m), head-to-tail

Weight: 25 pounds (11 kg)

Speed: Born to run on two feet as fast as 25 mph (40 kph). One expert suggests that Velly didn't run at all, but hopped like a kangaroo.

Special f/x (besides those claws): A stiff tail carried off the ground balanced Velly during its sprints and leaps. Also flicked the tail back and forth like a rudder when turning.

Best move: the Leap and Slash

Recommended sport: kickboxing

Sensory check: Long snout meant great sniffer. Eyes like a hawk's.

Brains: Big and wickedly smart

Chow time: All meat, no potatoes. Sharp saw-teeth and long jaw perfect for putting the quick bite on victims.

Lethal weapon: Need we say? These guys weren't big compared to other dinos—smaller than an adult human. But the middle claw on each hind foot was vicious, up to 5 razor-sharp centimeters long. To keep them sharp, Velly held the claws up when chasing prey. Once it caught up, the claws came down in slicing slashes.

Velly's fingernails were no picnic, either. Unlike its toe-claws, they worked like grappling hooks to get a firm grip on its victims.

Digs: Asia. Similar bones found in North America

Claim to fame: *Velociraptor* was *the* star of *Jurassic Park,* the movie. But some dino experts were *not* happy when director Steven Spielberg inflated the deadly dino to four times its actual size (making it even *nastier*). But then, some new bones cropped up in Utah. They were similar to a *Velociraptor*, all right, but with a slight difference: THEY WERE HUGE—*just like in the movie!* That shut most of the grumblers up, and the 20-foot-long (6 m), 1,000-pound (44 kg) killer with 11-inch-claws even got its own name: *Utahraptor.*

Death-Grip Fossil

Velociraptor doesn't just star in movies. One of the coolest fossils ever found shows a young Velly locked in mortal combat with a *Protoceratops*, a smaller cousin of *Triceratops*. When Velly attacked the frilled plant eater, Proto clamped onto its arm with its parrot-shaped beak. Velly, meanwhile, latched onto Proto's head with its other arm and planted a hind killer-claw into its belly. Sand covered and preserved the bones of the dukin' duo until they were discovered millions of years later, in 1971.

Not Guilty on All Charges

Despite its name, *Oviraptor* was not a true raptor. Though it munched meat and had huge claws, it was a bizarre beaked dinosaur with no teeth at all.

Oviraptor has just recently been declared innocent of being, as its name suggests, an "egg thief." The 1993 discovery in Mongolia of an adult *Oviraptor* skeleton covering at least 20 eggs proved that even meat eaters protected their young. It also suggested that the first *Oviraptor* ever found wasn't pilfering another dino's egg, but caring for its own.

Chapter 3

WHERE DID ALL THOSE DINOS GO?

If there's one thing dino experts don't agree on, it's how most of the last big dinosaurs finally got wiped out 65 million years ago. Some experts figure it happened in one big bang. Others say it took a while—maybe millions of years. It's the greatest unsolved mystery in the dino files. Here are just a few of the theories.

Please Don't Eat the Flowers

Plants with flowers didn't show up until the end of dino days. Before that, plant-eating dinos munched ferns and needlelike leaves. Could be that the dinos ate the newfangled flowers—and the flowers packed a poisonous punch. Once the plant eaters were gone, the meat chompers ate them.

Where's the Weather Channel When You Need It?

The world was mostly hot and steamy during the heyday of dinos. But fossils hint that the Earth chilled out about 65 million years ago. The chill would have zapped many tropical plants—the fave food of most dinos—as well.

Egg McDinosaur?

Dinos weren't the only critters crawling around during dino days. Rodentlike mammals were already scampering all over the place. Did these rascally varmints start making midnight snacks out of dinosaur eggs when mom and pop dinos were asleep? If so, and they got too good at it, well, that would surely have scrambled the dinos' future.

The "Could've Used Some Shades" Theory

You know ultraviolet light as the stuff that gives you sunburn. But dinos may have gotten more than red necks from catching too many UV rays. Some scientists think that increasing UV light was especially hard on dino eyeballs, causing cloudy lenses to form over them. This may have blinded the dinos so much that they couldn't find their food.

The No-Dino-Doo Dilemma

Fernlike plants were the favorite food of many dinosaurs. With good reason, too—they contained oils that kept food moving through the dinos' digestive tracts. When many types of ferns disappeared, it's possible that a lot of dinos croaked from chronic constipation. In other words, they got all plugged up!

Dante's Peaks

A bunch of volcanoes exploding at the same time

could have swamped dino land in bubbling hot lava. Those dinos that didn't fry might have starved to death, thanks to huge plumes of volcanic ash. The ash would have blocked the sun for months—or years—or wiped out Earth's protective ozone layer. This would have zapped most plant and animal life.

Great Ball of Fire!

The favorite theory of many experts is that a huge chunk of space rock slammed into the Earth, wiping out the dinos and lots of other living things. They say that the asteroid was 6–12 miles (9.6–19.2 km) wide and zoomed toward Earth at thousands of miles per hour. They've even pinpointed the crash site near Mexico's Yucatan Peninsula.

The evidence? A "fireball layer" containing asteroid bits showed up in a sample of rock 300 feet (90 m) beneath the ocean bed. Its age: exactly 65 million years old.

The favorite theory of many experts is that a huge chunk of space rock slammed into the Earth.

The asteroid itself vaporized in the intense heat. But it left a 180-mile-wide (288 m) crater. It also made a humongous mess of things. Tidal waves wiped out a bunch of plants and animals. And dust and debris in the air blocked the sun for months, chilling the planet and killing more life-forms. Altogether, the big bang may have nuked more than 70 percent of all species on Earth—including almost every dinosaur.

Chapter 4

THE FIRST BONE HUNTERS

It's hard to say when the very first dinosaur bones were dug up. People in China have been spying dino bones on the ground for more than 2,000 years. And all those stories about fire-breathing dragons from the Middle Ages? Good chance they started after someone tripped over a dino bone or two. In fact, in the late 1600s, the huge thigh bone of a *Megalosaurus* was put in one British museum and declared to be the leg bone of a human giant!

The very first bone to score a proper dino i.d. was picked up by Mary Ann Mantell in 1822. She was strolling in Sussex, England, when she spotted a weird, flat-shaped tooth. Her fossil-collecting husband, Dr. Gideon Mantell, decided the tooth belonged to a huge plant-eating reptile from Cretaceous times. He named it *Iguanodon*.

Nearly twenty years later, Sir Richard Owen,

another British scientist, announced that *Iguanodons* were just one kind of *dinosaur*, or "terrible lizard," that once lived all over the world.

Dinomania was born.

The Great Bone War

The two biggest stars of the earliest dino-hunting days, Edward Drinker Cope and O. C. Marsh, hated each other's guts.

Marsh had big-money family ties and was head of Yale University's Peabody Museum. Cope had money, too, as well as a top position at the Academy of Natural Sciences in Philadelphia.

The friction started when Cope discovered Marsh secretly paying Cope's helpers to ship their fossil finds to Marsh. Then Marsh embarrassed Cope by publicly showing that Cope had stuck the skull of one ancient critter on the butt end of its skeleton. That plunged the two scientists into a bitter battle to see who could dig up more dinosaurs.

In the late 1870s, Marsh and Cope and their crews ventured to America's Wild West in search of big bones. The crews spied on each other's camps and tried to keep their own digs secret. They even "rustled" bones from each other's camps, then took credit for their "discoveries."

In their frenzy to outdo one another, Marsh and Cope often gave different names to many of the same dinosaur species. (This confused scientists for the next century.)

> # The crews spied on each other's camps and tried to keep their own digs secret.

Meanwhile, the pugnacious paleontologists made daily newspaper headlines, and average Americans followed their fight. When the dust had settled, the feuding fossil finders and their field crews had discovered 136 new dinosaurs (of only 287 dino species known at the time)!

Edward Drinker Cope, 1840–1897

Edward Drinker Cope seemed more at home at his

dusty dinosaur digs in the American West than in his Philadelphia Museum office. Even the threat of attacking Indians didn't stop him and his crew from their hunt for dino bones. They arrived in Montana just after the Battle of the Little Bighorn. That's where General Custer and his 7th Cavalry were wiped out by Chief Sitting Bull and his Sioux warriors. Cope figured his timing was perfect: the chief and his tribe would hardly be waiting around for the U.S. Army, which was looking for them.

By the time he died, Cope and his team had named more than 1,200 new animal species, including 56 dinosaurs. His biggest dino finds: *Camarasaurus* and *Coelophysis*.

Orthniel Charles Marsh, 1831–1899

"O. C." Marsh didn't jump into science until

On at least one of his trips, he was joined by sharp-shooter Buffalo Bill Cody.

he was 25. (His younger classmates at Yale University called him "Daddy.") Later he talked a rich uncle into donating a museum to Yale, and Marsh took charge of it. One of his goals: to fill it with dinosaurs.

Marsh and his crew made three big bone-digging journeys to the Wild West between 1870 and 1872, when the U.S. and Native Americans were still at war. On at least one of his trips, he was joined by sharpshooter Buffalo Bill Cody. Marsh then spent most of his time back at his museum putting the dino bones together. He also hired a gang of field workers to continue digging for him. Some of the most famous dinos Marsh named, such as *Stegosaurus* and *Triceratops*, were found by his assistants. His other big finds: *Apatosaurus, Allosaurus,* and *Diplodocus.* Marsh named 80 new dinos in his career.

Earl Douglass, 1862–1931

Earl Douglass dug bones for Pittsburgh's Carnegie Museum of Natural History from 1902 until 1924. He discovered the Carnegie Quarry, a massive Jurassic graveyard near the small town of Jenson, Utah. He dug at the site, one of the world's richest bone beds, for 15 years. To haul his big-boned skeletons out of Utah's rocky deserts, Douglass used horse-drawn wagons. Since those days, the quarry has coughed up more than 5,000 bones and parts of more than 400 individual dinos. Some have been left stuck in the walls of the quarry—with a museum built around it. Douglass pushed to preserve the place as "Dinosaur National Monument," now visited by 500,000 dino lovers each year.

Barnum Brown, 1873–1963

Barnum Brown, a.k.a. "Mr. Bones," worked for the American Museum of Natural History in New York City for 66 years. He had a knack for pinpointing dino bones in the wildest of places, but didn't dress like an "Indiana Jones." He was known instead for his stylin' full-length fur coat and his gold-tipped cane—even out in the digs!

To search for bones in Canada's hilly and hard-to-get-to Alberta badlands, Brown made a river barge his base. He cruised the Red Deer River, stopping wherever he thought bones lurked. Almost always he hit pay dirt. He'd load the barge with the big bones and float them to the nearest railway station. The dinos hopped the next train to New York.

Mr. Bones found more dinos during his career than any dino hunter before him. They included *Tyrannosaurus rex* and *Dromeosaurus*, the first raptor ever dug up.

Roy Chapman Andrews, 1884–1960

Indiana Jones, move over. Roy Chapman Andrews was the real thing. When he led his research teams from the American Museum of Natural History into Asia's toughest terrain (five different times), he sported a slick felt hat and high leather boots. He also toted a revolver. Andrews's teams used five cars and dozens of two-humped camels to explore Mongolia's badlands. They plowed through sandstorms, battled bandits, and skirted war zones. When they first hit the dino jackpot, dinosaurs weren't even what they were after. Andrews was most interested in ancient *human* remains.

Andrews uncovered the bones of the largest mammal ever, the rhinolike *Indricotherium*. He also discovered the first proof ever that dinosaurs laid eggs in large nests. Oh, and he found the first bones of *Oviraptor* and *Velociraptor*, too.

Chapter 5

DINO HUNTERS TODAY!

When you get right down to it, there's not a whole lot of difference between bone hunters today and those of a hundred years ago. Same torturous terrain in mostly far-off places. Same sizzling temperatures and biting sandstorms. Same bloodsucking insects and frightful wild animals. Even, occasionally, the same exploding war zones.

Today's paleontologists still hunt for bones, inch by lonely inch, often walking for hours, days, or weeks without a find. And they still use a lot of the same old digging tools: picks, chisels, whisk brooms, and shovels. They even camp out in tents like the old-timers.

Not that some of today's dino hunters haven't added their own modern twists. A few have discovered brand-new dinosaurs without ever going on an outdoor expedition. They dig in the basements of museums for overlooked bones in storage. Others have begun using high-tech gadgets to help them pinpoint their fossil treasures.

There are *hundreds* of cool bone hunters out there digging up dinos. There are hundreds more scientists who work behind the scenes, cleaning and studying these bones. Keep all of these dino experts in mind as you read next about some of the top bone hunters in North America.

Dr. Bob Bakker: The Bad Boy of Bones

Bob Bakker is a freelance paleontologist, movie consultant, writer, and lecturer.

Even before finishing his first stint in college, Bob was shaking up the dinosaur world with his wild ideas. In the late '60s, he stated that some dinos were warm-blooded and quick on their feet—the total opposite of what most dino experts believed. Then, in 1974, he suggested that our fine-feathered friends, the birds, are actually the latest version of dinosaurs—another idea that caused a flap in dino circles. Now, both of Bob's outlaw theories are accepted by many paleontologists, and Bob continues to churn out new brainstorms.

He also finds new dinosaurs. He named one of his latest discoveries *Drinker*, after Edward Drinker Cope, the famous dino hunter of the late 1800s. Drinker, the smallest plant-eating dino ever found, could fit inside a chicken egg. "That would be a safe pet," Bob says.

Bob has dug dino bones for thirty years, written several feisty dinosaur books, and helped on the movies *Jurassic Park* and *The Lost World*. In fact, Michael Crichton, the author of the novels, says Bob's ideas inspired his book.

Quote: "Dinosaurs are nature's special effects."

Dr. Karen Chin: The Whole Poop on Dinosaurs

Karen is a visiting scientist with the U.S. Geological Survey in northern California.

Meet the world's top expert on coprolites, a.k.a. dinosaur dung, a.k.a. fossilized doo-doo. That's right, poop.

Dino doo unlocks the secrets of what dinosaurs ate.

"Nobody has ever done an exhaustive study on coprolites," Karen says. "Most geologists wouldn't want to put their names on it."

Karen doesn't seem to mind. To her, dino doo unlocks the secrets of what dinosaurs ate. The coprolites of meat-eatin' dinos, for example, are often speckled white. Those specks are bone fragments of the dinos that got chomped.

How does Karen know when she's eyeing a real dinosaur chip? "It looks like poop," she says. "That's it. It looks like poop."

Dr. Philip Currie: Canada's Hunter of the Hunters

Phil is the Curator of Dinosaurs at the Royal Tyrrell Museum in Alberta, Canada.

Phil knows meat-eating dinosaurs like no other scientist

in the world. Hand him a meat chomper's tooth, and he'll tell you exactly which prehistoric predator took a bite with it. That expertise has led Phil all over the world in search of dino bones, as well as to help other dino hunters i.d. their finds.

Not that Phil has to travel far from his own home base to dig up big bones. He's the boss at the Royal Tyrrell Museum in Drumheller, Alberta. His favorite digs are 120 miles away in the badlands of Alberta, now called Dinosaur Provincial Park. Early in his career, Phil realized that none of the region's 300 dug-up dinos were on display in Alberta. He led the charge to build the Royal Tyrrell Museum. Opened in 1986, it now boasts the largest collection of mounted dinosaurs in the world.

Dr. Jack Horner: Good Papa Paleontologist

Jack is Curator of Paleontology at the Museum of the Rockies, Bozeman, Montana.

In 1978 Jack and his friend Bob Makela went hunting for

bones in Montana. They found zip in the field. Then the owners of a rock shop asked Jack to i.d. some tiny bones they'd stored in a coffee can. EUREKA! *That's* where they struck it rich.

The bones led to the discovery of a whole nestful of dino eggs. And *that* led to a whole colony of dino *nests*.

The dino nest eggs gave Jack a new idea—that some dinosaurs took good care of their young 'uns. He named the nesting dino *Maiasaura*, or "Good Mother Lizard." And the Good Mother has been delivering more buried treasure ever since.

In 1981, when one of Jack's crew members tried to plant a tent stake, he hit bones. The whole crew had been camping on an enormous dino graveyard! Jack guesses that "Camposaur Quarry" is the biggest bone bed in the world, and that more than 10,000 *Maiasaura* skeletons are buried there.

The whole crew had been camping on an enormous dino graveyard!

In 1983, Jack and his crew found the first fossilized dinosaur eggs with the babies (called "embryos") still inside them. Better yet, in 1988, Jack uncovered a fossilized nest of dinosaur babies caught in the act of hatching from their eggs!

Drs. Mike Novacek and Mark Norell: The Gobi Brothers

Mike is the Curator and Dean of Science at the American Museum of Natural History (AMNH). Mark is the museum's Assistant Curator.

Before 1990, thanks to ugly politics, Mongolia's enormous Gobi Desert had been off-limits to U.S. and other Western scientists for sixty years. Too bad, because Roy Chapman Andrews had discovered absolutely amazing bone beds there in the 1920s. But when the rules changed recently, Mike and Mark were two of the first Americans to blaze across the Gobi again.

Despite blistering sandstorms, 110-degree heat, and broken-down vehicles, the two AMNH paleontologists and their international team made the trip several times. In 1993, they stumbled upon a former oasis

> ## Many seemed to have been preserved exactly, as if buried alive in a stupendous sandstorm.

bristling with dino bones. Many seemed to have been preserved exactly, as if buried alive in a stupendous sandstorm.

One skeleton, an 8-foot-long (2.4 m) *Oviraptor,* was caught in the act of covering her twenty eggs with her arms. That showed for the first time that some meat-eating dinos watched over their kids like birds do today.

M & M also discovered an *Oviraptor* egg containing one of the few complete embryos of a meat-eating dino ever found.

And finally, a young adult *Velociraptor* was dug up with a small hole in its forehead. Mark found another Velly tooth that fit perfectly into the hole. His theory: *Velociraptors,* who usually ripped into other dinos for dinner, could be pretty nasty to each other, as well.

Dr. John Ostrom:
Warm Blood and Switchblade Toes

John is the retired head of paleontology at Yale University's Peabody Museum.

On the last day of a summer dig in 1964, John spied a perfect claw sticking out of a steep Montana slope. But he knew this was no ordinary dinosaur weapon. It belonged to a whole new family of meat eaters known as *raptors*.

John named his raptor *Deinonychus*, or "terrible claw," and headed back to Montana for the rest of its bones the next year. What he found: a whole pack of these dinos with switchblade toes.

John's study of the quick-footed Terrible Claw got him to thinking that some dinos *had* to be warm-blooded. (That's because cold-blooded reptiles can't move very fast for long periods of time.) In 1969, ideas like that were still pushing the envelope of paleontology. Now, thanks to John and his former student Bob Bakker, it's old news.

> But he knew this was no ordinary dinosaur weapon. It belonged to a whole new family of meat eaters known as raptors.

Dr. Paul Sereno: "Illinois" Jones

Paul is Associate Professor of Paleontology and Evolution at the University of Chicago.

Paul is one of the hottest young paleontologists digging up dinosaurs today. In just ten years, Paul and his team have dug up the bones of at least four "new" dinos.

In '91, he found dog-sized *Eoraptor* in Argentina—a granddaddy of dinos. In 1993, despite bandits, 115-degree heat, and civil war, he dusted off *Afrovenator* ("African hunter")—a 30-foot-long (9 m) carnivore hidden beneath Africa's Sahara sands. There, he also scooped out a 60-foot-long (18 m) plant eater still not named.

In 1995, Paul was back in the Sahara. After days in scorching heat—even using old tire bits to pad worn boots—his team struck dino gold again: *Carcharodontosaurus*, or "Shark-Toothed Reptile." The only other bones found of this mega meat chomper had been destroyed in World War II.

Then, to top *that* off, Paul's team stumbled upon *Deltadromeus agilis*, a.k.a. "agile delta runner." This lean, mean, flesh-eating machine also lived 90 million years ago.

Paul figures out what a place looked like millions of years ago by chomping mouthfuls of dirt. He feels and listens to how gritty the soil is against his teeth. "The bigger the sand particles," he says, "the closer you are, more or less, to a river basin." He spits out the dirt when he's through.

Quote: "We're just scratching the surface of a dinosaur world that's waiting to be unearthed."

DINOS ALIVE?

In the motion picture *Baby*, a couple learns how much work a baby *Brontosaurus* can be.

The coolest news about dinos in the last twenty years? They weren't completely wiped out. Most paleontologists today agree that birds are directly descended, or related to, some types of dinosaurs. Surely you've heard of Scotland's Loch Ness Monster, which some people believe is actually a plesiosaur, a distant swimming cousin of dinos. And in deepest Africa, some people claim that a giant Sauropod—similar to *Apatosaurus*—still roams the jungles. (They call it "Mokele Membe," and it's the mystery creature who inspired the dino movie *Baby*.)

Meanwhile, the super-great-grandchildren of a few critters alive at the time of the dinosaurs are still kicking today with few, if any, improvements. Cockroaches have munched their way through the ages since dino times.

> # Cockroaches have munched their way through the ages since dino times.

Some crocodiles and turtles have hardly changed at all. And young Hoatzin birds of South American jungles still sport claws on their wing tips—like the old-time *Archaeopteryx* and the pterosaurs. (The Hoatzin's claws disappear as it gets older.) Sharks are dino-era survivors, as are jellyfish, spiders, starfish, horseshoe crabs, and dragonflies.

As for bringing dinos back to life the way the dino-crazy scientist did in *Jurassic Park*, well . . . not likely, say most scientists. Recent studies show that the DNA found in current dino fossils is way too old and damaged ever to be jump-started into a living, roaring dino—even if new DNA technology could make such a thing possible. (DNA is the code in our cells that determines how we look and act.)

Then again, scientists in Scotland recently created a whole new sheep named Dolly from a single cell of another sheep. (This is called "cloning.") And the DNA of ancient bugs caught in amber (the sap of some trees) is preserved almost perfectly. Could there be an unfound chunk of some dino out there trapped in amberlike stuff, with its DNA still fresh?

If so, who knows what the future holds? And just in case, turn the page. . . .

Chapter 7

DINO SURVIVAL GUIDE

Okay, okay. Dinosaurs were wiped out 65 million years ago—and humans didn't show up for another 63 million years. But suppose you hop a time machine back to dino days, or some mad scientist *does* bring dinosaurs back using their DNA.

Here are a few tips to help you get along:

• Watch where you walk.

You think stepping into doggie-doo is the pits? How about a mound of prehistoric poop as large as a beach ball? That's what you'd find *everywhere* around you. The largest, mushiest mounds are from humongous plant eaters

But if you plow into a torpedo-shaped dino chip speckled white, better check your back: those are from meat chompers, and those specks are bone bits!

such as *Brachiosaurus*. But if you plow into a torpedo-shaped dino chip speckled white, better check your back: those are from meat chompers, and those specks are bone bits!

• Egg over-easy?

Think again. Those bread-loaf-size eggs you're planning to fry up are no ordinary chicken's. Those are dinos waiting to hatch. More important than that—their parents can be mighty protective. You wouldn't want to be caught rustling up their babies-to-be for breakfast.

• Think twice before you bring home that stray. . . .

Most dinos start out as cute little fellas. But they grow at *astonishing* rates. And who knows what you'd wind up with? A big plant eater would eat you out of house and home in a hurry. A meat eater, well, would probably eat *you*.

• . . . But if you must have a pet . . .

Pick up a dino named Drinker at your prehistoric pet store. Drinker could fit inside a chicken egg. It mostly munches leaves, though an insect here and there wouldn't hurt.

• Watch where you take a dip. . . .

Sure, fish-breath *Baryonyx* might take a swipe at you in the drink. And sharks also cruised prehistoric waters. But the real danger is when you step out to dry. The shorelines of lakes, rivers, and seas were freeways for whole herds of plant-eating dinos—and the packs of predators that stalked them. One of these mega-trackways stretches hundreds of miles between Colorado and New Mexico, and is partly buried beneath the city of Denver. It contains billions of dino tracks (though only a few thousand are visible).

• . . . And look before you climb that tree!

Velociraptor, the star flesh ripper of *Jurassic Park*, could claw its way to the top of a tree. (Lousy swimmer, though.)

• Please don't feed the animals.

That friendly plant-eating *Edmontosaurus* might snap up the greens you offer like a pony plucking carrots from your fingers. But if it pulled in a finger or two by mistake, well, it's too ugly to think about. This dino had *1,400* diamond-shaped grinders for back teeth.

• Be unseen and be uneaten.

Most dinosaurs, especially the meat-hunting variety, have eyes like an eagle's, forward-looking and sharp. They also see in Technicolor. To avoid becoming a dino dinner, dress in clothes that are the color of the scene around you (green in the woods, brown in the desert). Then again, most dinos could smell you a mile away. Not much you can do about *that*.

• Don't go by the book.

You're dino-watching with your *Field Guide to Cretaceous Critters* when a toothy carnivore starts eyeing you back. Its teeth, tail, and tiny hands fit the book's description of *T. rex*, but what's that big flap of skin hanging from its cheeks? *Don't* wait around to find out.

Dino experts today can only *guess* at what dinos looked like millions of years ago, based mostly on their bones. But other parts of them, such as skin flaps, trunks, humps, fur, and feathers would have rotted away completely.

No one really knows what colors dinos were, either. In the old days, most paleontologists painted their dinos dull gray or brown. These days, the experts are adding splashes from every color in the rainbow. Reason: they figure dinos developed brighter colors for the same reasons some of today's birds and other animals have: to blend in with their backgrounds, to rule their roosts, or to attract mates.

The point is, some dinos may look nothing like we think they do!

Investigator's Field Kit

S ome of the most important fossil finds ever were not made by dino experts. Hikers stumbled upon the skeleton of *Seismosaurus* in New Mexico, for example. A farmer found the first bones in a new treasure trove of dino fossils in China. And recently, three-year-old David Shiffler, also from New Mexico, used his toy tractor to dig up a fossilized eggshell. Turns out it came from a meat-eating dino—and was the first of its kind!

Not everyone gets so lucky, of course. But following these simple tips can help turn *you* into a successful fossil hunter.

What to Take Dino Hunting

- Geological hammer
- Steel chisel
- Safety goggles
- 10-X (power) hand lens (a.k.a. magnifying glass)
- Compass and maps
- Newspaper, cotton, plastic sandwich bags, and matchboxes (for holding your fossils)
- Whisk broom, plus steel or plastic brushes (an old toothbrush works)
- Notepad, pencil, pen, and masking tape (for labels and notes)
- Sunblock
- Filled water bottle or canteen
- Trail food or lunch
- Work gloves
- Bug repellent
- Mini first-aid kit

1. Look for the layers.

Most fossils show up in sedimentary rock—layers of rock pressed together to give you that slick, striped look—such as limestone. You might find outcrops of sedimentary rock where a road cuts through a hill or where cliffs jut out.

Rocks and pebbles at the beach or in streams might contain fossils, too. Chunks of coal or slabs of slate (used for old-time chalkboards) are also good fossil hideouts.

2. Chip away.

Use a geological hammer and steel chisel to chip around the fossil about one inch. Break the chunk out of the rock and wrap it in plastic or paper.

3. Take notes.

Number your fossils and write down exactly where you found them. That way you can track down more later.

4. Back at the lab . . .

When you hit home, look hard at your fossil rock. Can you tell where the rock ends and the fossil begins? Use a penknife or needle to scrape away the rocky edges. Use a toothbrush or steel bristles to brush off what's left.

5. Bathtime

Soap up your fossil and rinse it off. Dry it with a soft towel. Check out a library book or two on identifying fossils, and try to name your treasure. Now add it to your personal museum!

A Kid Fossil Hunter's Code of Honor

• Always let an adult tag along on your fossil-finding missions.

• Never dig fossils on private land without permission from the owner.

• Before hunting for fossils in parks or other public places, check the laws to see what you're allowed to dig or take out. In some places, rare fossils such as dino bones can only be dug up by experts.

• If you find a large fossil, mark the spot and report it to park officials or a local museum. Let a scientist check it out.

• Chip only at rocks showing hints of fossils. Don't crack rocks just for the fun of it.

• When chipping rocks, wear safety goggles.

• Clean chipped rocks and debris from your work area, and from roads and footpaths.

• Be careful! Always be on the lookout for:

-rock slides or ledges that might break

-dangerous animals such as rattlesnakes, bears, or cougars

-beehives

-bad weather (lightning, sandstorms, flash floods, cold temperatures)

HOT DINO DISPLAYS

There are *hundreds* of museums with sizzling dino displays, so you can probably find one near you! The following are a few of the hottest to check out, if you get a chance. (And if you don't, do the next best thing: hit their websites.)

American Museum of Natural History
79th Street at Central Park West
New York, NY 10024
(212) 769-5000
On the Web: http://www.amnh.org
One of the world's ultimate fossil collections—completely reassembled to show off more than 100 big-boned dinos.

Carnegie Museum of Natural History
4400 Forbes Ave.
Pittsburgh, PA 15213
(412) 622-3131
On the Web: http://www.clpgh.org/cmnh/
Here you can *smell* the world of dinosaurs, watch actors play old-time dino hunters, and see what goes into fixing up old bones for viewing.

Royal Tyrrell Museum of Paleontology
Box 7500

Highway 838, Midland Provincial Park
Drumheller, Alberta T0J 0Y0 Canada
1-888-440-4240
On the Web: http://www.tyrrell.magtech.ab.ca
This is a kingly collection of more than 200 dino skeletons. Many are from digs around the museum and Dinosaur Provincial Park, just 120 miles away. You can even get down and dirty at a real dig hiding 68-million-year-old bones. Hot tip: send an electronic postcard to a friend from the museum's website.

Dinosaur National Monument
4545 Highway 40
Dinosaur, CO 81610-9724
(970) 374-3000
On the Web: http://www.nps.gov/dino/
This place is *really* hot—it's in a desert. In 1909, paleontologists found a riverbed full of dino bones. One part became the wall of a visitor center—with *1,600* dino bones sticking out. More than 5,000 bones have been dug up so far.

Museum of the Rockies
Montana State University
Bozeman, MT 59717
(406) 994-2251
Here is one place you can see dinos still inside their eggs—and the experts working on them.

Other great dino museums include: The Field Museum, Chicago, IL; Dinosaur State Park, Rocky Hill, CT; Academy of Natural Sciences, Philadelphia, PA; North Carolina Museum of Life and Sciences, Durham, NC; Lawrence Hall of Science, University of California at Berkeley, CA; Science Museum of Minnesota, St. Paul, MN; Royal Ontario Museum, Toronto, Ontario (Canada); and the National Museum of Natural Sciences, Ottawa, Ontario (Canada).